Dear Parents:

Congratulations! Your child is taking the first steps on an exciting journey. The destination? Independent reading!

STEP INTO READING® will help your child get there. The program offers five steps to reading success. Each step includes fun stories and colorful art or photographs. In addition to original fiction and books with favorite characters, there are Step into Reading Non-Fiction Readers, Phonics Readers and Boxed Sets, Sticker Readers, and Comic Readers—a complete literacy program with something to interest every child.

Learning to Read, Step by Step!

Ready to Read   Preschool–Kindergarten
• big type and easy words • rhyme and rhythm • picture clues
For children who know the alphabet and are eager to begin reading.

Reading with Help   Preschool–Grade 1
• basic vocabulary • short sentences • simple stories
For children who recognize familiar words and sound out new words with help.

Reading on Your Own   Grades 1–3
• engaging characters • easy-to-follow plots • popular topics
For children who are ready to read on their own.

Reading Paragraphs   Grades 2–3
• challenging vocabulary • short paragraphs • exciting stories
For newly independent readers who read simple sentences with confidence.

Ready for Chapters   Grades 2–4
• chapters • longer paragraphs • full-color art
For children who want to take the plunge into chapter books but still like colorful pictures.

STEP INTO READING® is designed to give every child a successful reading experience. The grade levels are only guides; children will progress through the steps at their own speed, developing confidence in their reading.

Remember, a lifetime love of reading starts with a single step!

Published in the United States by Random House Children's Books, a division of Penguin Random House LLC, 1745 Broadway, New York, NY 10019, and in Canada by Penguin Random House Canada Limited, Toronto.

Step into Reading, Random House, and the Random House colophon are registered trademarks of Penguin Random House LLC.

Visit us on the Web!
StepIntoReading.com
rhcbooks.com

Educators and librarians, for a variety of teaching tools, visit us at RHTeachersLibrarians.com

ISBN 978-1-5247-6911-6 (trade) — ISBN 978-1-5247-6912-3 (lib. bdg.)

Printed in the United States of America
10 9 8 7 6 5 4 3 2 1

Random House Children's Books supports the First Amendment and celebrates the right to read.

Barbie YOU CAN BE a Soccer Player

by Kristen L. Depken
illustrated by Dynamo Limited
based on the story by Devra Newberger Speregen

Random House 🏠 New York

Barbie gets ready
for a big soccer game.

Stacie helps
Barbie find her
shin guards.

She wishes
Barbie a good game.

Barbie meets her team
on the field.
They stretch.
They warm up.

Coach brings
a soccer star
named Lucy
to the game.
She will help the coach.

The game starts.

Raquelle kicks the ball.

Barbie runs

toward the goal.

Barbie is open.

But Raquelle does not

pass to her.

The team takes a break.
Coach tells them
to work together.
Raquelle does not listen.

The game starts again.
The ball goes
out of bounds.
Barbie will make
a corner kick.

Barbie kicks the ball.

She runs back

onto the field.

Lucy cheers for her.

Raquelle gets the ball.
She kicks it
past two players.
She scores a goal!

Barbie's team wins!
They hug and cheer.
Raquelle is upset.
She thinks *she* won
the game,
not the team.

Lucy tells Barbie they
played a great game.

The next day,
Barbie practices
with Lucy's team.

Lucy's teammate
has a great kick!
They work as a team
to win the game.

Later, Lucy tells
Barbie and her team
to work together.

The girls listen—
except Raquelle.
She does not think
she needs help.

The girls start a game.
Raquelle will not pass.
A player steals the ball
from her.

The ball goes
out of bounds.
Barbie kicks it
to Raquelle.

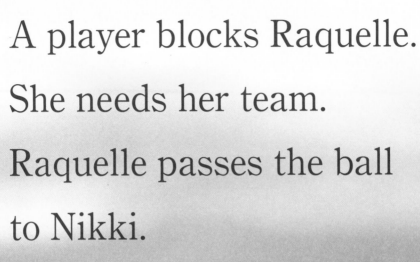

A player blocks Raquelle.
She needs her team.
Raquelle passes the ball
to Nikki.

Nikki scores a goal!

Their team wins!

"Great teamwork!"

Lucy cheers.

"You can be

a great soccer player!"